Science Fiction and Alternate History—a Collection of Short Stories

By David K Scholes

Strategic Book Publishing
New York, NewYork

Strategic Book Publishing
An imprint of AEG Publishing Group
845 Third Avenue, 6th Floor – 6016
New York, NY 10022
www.eloquentbooks.com

ISBN: 978-1-60693-885-0   1-60693-855-1

Printed in the United States of America

Book Design: D. Johnson, Dedicated Business Solutions, Inc.

Table of Contents

Science Fiction and Alternate History—a Collection of Short Stories

The (Second) Battle of Britain

Kent, England, August 2025

Over one hundred thousand feet above the gentle English countryside the alien fighter crafts were returning to their mother ship after a punishing raid on the British capital. The Drell did not expect to be troubled at this altitude. Earth's reserves of ground launched high altitude anti-aircraft missiles and anti-missile missiles were virtually non existent. Also the altitude was considered too high for Earth's few remaining fighters.

Suddenly screaming in from above them at mach three point five, an aircraft new to the aliens came. British Aerospace's superlative "All England" interceptor fighter. The RAF's pride and joy often referred to as just the AE appeared out of nowhere. Its latest generation stealth characteristics enabled it to avoid the alien detection systems.

Squadron leaders Stu Dowding and Jennifer Leigh-Mallory led the charge as the RAF ripped the unsuspecting alien fighters to shreds. It didn't end there as the two squadrons then launched a coordinated long range missile attack against the alien base ship in a low geosynchronous orbit above the North Sea. Unfortunately the base ships force shields held. This time. However the only alien base ship above the British Isles was moved into a much higher geosynchronous orbit well out into the Atlantic. A direct consequence of the attack.

So began in August 2025 the second Battle of Britain, a struggle of significance for human history equal to the first.

When they first arrived, the aliens had concluded that their main opposition would come from the populous large land masses and large industrial concentrations in such countries as China, India, Brazil, the United States, and Russia. These were the areas they sought to ground down and subjugate. Unlike the fictitious Martians of HG Wells famous novel, these real-life aliens had been slow to recognize the strategic significance of the British Isles. They had been even slower to recognize the intense military professionalism of its armed forces. By the time they did, the alien Drell were on the wane.

The battle raged on into September. Very early in the conflict the RAF withdrew all of its ageing Eurofighter Typhoons. Regrettably even its few F22 Raptors, purchased from the Americans, had also to be withdrawn. Both fighters were hopelessly outclassed in speed, agility, stealth capabilities, ceiling, and firepower by the compact and rather nasty alien fighters. The aliens struck across the length and breadth of the British Isles, even Eire. With no significant ground to air missiles left in its inventory, the burden of the air defense of Great Britain and Ireland fell squarely on the new fighter.

There was some assistance from the Royal Navy's remaining two super carriers, the 125,000 ton King George V and the Rodney. Unfortunately the HMS Southampton had been sunk in the battle of New York many months ago. The carriers were still equipped with some anti-aircraft and anti-missile capabilities. More importantly both ships had a small number of the naval equivalent of the All England fighter on board. The alien's inability to sink either of these two leviathans, not for want of trying, was a major mistake on their part.

In general the aliens came in hard and fast from their base ship and at such speeds that they were difficult to intercept on their descent run towards the British Isles. Their weaponry included a combination of powerful lasers and ultra high-rate-of-fire sub-nuclear projectiles On their return to the base ship, though, the aliens were vulnerable. They were consistently frustrated by the RAF's ability to attack them, even at altitudes well above one hundred thousand feet. With the Brit pilots often coming in from above, alien losses were quite simply staggering.

How did the pilots of the fast and highly maneuverable alien fighters react when first encountering the new AE fighter? Had they felt as the young Luftwaffe pilots had more than eighty-five years ago when they encountered their first spitfires? Or perhaps the aliens were just too brutal to care. The mild qualitative edge afforded the RAF by the magnificent fighter was a little further enhanced by the quality of the RAF pilots defending their homeland.

On the day of September 15, 2025, the fighting was particularly grueling. The aliens seemed to send everything they had at London in particular. The great city was ablaze. The RAF was out in force, and pilots were particularly eager to see that none of the alien fighters returned to their base ship that day. Very few of them actually did.

After five confirmed kills to his credit and preparing to return to the new Tittington air base, Squadron Leader Dowding moved down to a much lower altitude. For a moment he thought his eyes were playing tricks on him as he flew over an old Luftwaffe Heinkel bomber, damaged and being pursued by an RAF Hawker Hurricane. At still lower altitude Dowding saw a huge stream of variously damaged German bombers limping towards the English Channel. Spitfires and Hurricanes were on their tail. Somehow, briefly, Dowding had been able to look through a window in time to exactly eighty-five years ago when another great victory had been won. It left him both humble and elated and with renewed determination.

The next day the aliens didn't come. They didn't come the day after that either, or the next day. Eventually there would be more attacks on the British Isles. The aliens had not been beaten yet. Later though, it would be possible to identify September fifteenth as the crucial turning point.

Several weeks later the RAF mounted a successful attack on the alien base ship. The new high altitude long range Scotland Bombers were escorted by two full squadrons of AE fighters. The bombers extremely long range air-to-air missiles (ELRAAMs) were equipped with the last nuclear warheads available in the British Isles. Not all of the missiles got through, but enough of them did to defeat the base ship force shields and vaporize it.

The new British Prime Minister was exultant at the news. He had been down to Portsmouth to review the preparations for the planned trip to the east coast of America by the HMS King George V carrier battle group. All formal contact with the American military had been lost as it seemed to have dissolved into chaos. Still there were plenty of informal contacts and the nation persisted in resisting the aliens in various ways. The little that was known of the situation in New York City was not encouraging.

Theodore Winston Tittington knew that the aliens had to break the British in their Island in order to win the war. He also now knew deep within himself that the Drell could no longer do this.

With victory in the second battle of Britain, the time had come to see what help could be rendered for old and less fortunate allies.

Grey Power

Greater Los Angeles, 2069

The feral youth was running in overdrive. He'd taken some sort of booster drug, possibly boostein. His eyes bulged, his heart thumped, and his arms and legs pumped away like pistons. The adrenalin poured through his system aided by the booster drug.

Two of the elite police managed to keep pace with him. The third individual, somewhat older, came along a bit slower but still kept them in body radar contact.

The police seemed to have no difficulty in keeping up with the desperate hyped up youth. He guessed they were wearing the latest model Carl Lewis exo-skeleton units, hardly detectable and with considerably enhanced performance from earlier models. He could be drugged up to the eyeballs with boostein and still not outrun them or out jump them for that matter. What he wouldn't give for five minutes use of one of those units.

The police moved in—their taser effect guns on the maim setting. At the last moment both of them moved their taser settings to mild stun. The youth went crashing to the ground almost instantly. When he saw the "maim," the individual attached to the police unit came up faster than expected. He was wearing the instantly recognizable yellow arm band of a Grey Power adviser. "Got the little turd." Then he called out, "Well done chaps!"

"What's he done?" asked an inquisitive elderly passer-by.

"The worst," said the adviser "crime 534B."

"So why's he still moving," yelled the passer-by indignantly. "He should be dead or at least significantly maimed."

The Grey Power adviser looked at his two colleagues in an accusatory manner. "He's got a point there; what the hell's going on here?"

The two younger cops looked at the adviser. He realized the taser effect guns must have been put on mild stun; it was the only explanation for the arrogant youth's relatively quick recovery. He would have to report the matter for disciplinary proceedings against the officers. He couldn't possibly let this pass.

Since 2055 the presence of Grey Power advisers was mandatory on all major police call-outs in greater Los Angeles, as it was with most police forces anywhere in the world. And lord knows the demographics were such that there were plenty of volunteers for the advisory positions.

The adviser made his formal complaint. The police disciplinary board had to take it seriously. If not, they knew he would take it further, even to Grey Power itself. Lord knows even Governments didn't want to upset that all-nations' organization that represented the vast population and financial power of most people in the world who were over fifty-five.

In keying in his complaint the adviser provided all the electronic evidence related to the crime 534B. Visuals included exact time of offence from his eye camera implant, sound from his ear receptors, etc. Surprisingly, even in that age he had to actually voice in the offence. The alpha numeric designation wasn't enough. "Crime 534B—loitering within fifty meters of an aged persons' retirement village and playing loud music," he stated to the computer. Then he shuddered involuntarily. There was just no respect among the youth of today. What were the two officers thinking when they merely stunned the miscreant?

The British Are Coming

Somewhere in the Bronx, New York City, Late September 2025

The four men entered the large basement area. Even among this tough gathering of ex-truckers and bikers they seemed to stand out. Their purpose was to gather information and organize resistance to the aliens. Also they were to prepare the way if the shock troops came.

Much the same thing was taking place in various parts of the other boroughs of New York City. Four-man Special Air Service (SAS) and Special Boat Squad (SBS) teams were trying to establish an overall picture of the situation. A while back submarines had landed the operatives.

A confused picture emerged. Organized resistance by the U.S. military had effectively ceased, at least hereabouts. However, some military men were among the well armed gangs and other groups still resisting the Drell. The aliens were hardly the winners. Individual alien military units were still operating, but there was no cohesion between the different small units. The SAS saw that something was needed to break the deadlock. Otherwise the battle for New York could go on forever.

The destruction in the city was frightful. Even the steel tough SAS and SBS were taken aback by it. The few aerial reconnaissance shots had not told the full picture.

The vital question: Should this place, once the greatest city on Earth, be saved? Or should modest British resources be used elsewhere? That vital decision was being made in London even as the SAS went about their business.

Newfoundland, Canada, Late September 2025

The big Nimrod-Three maritime surveillance aircraft touched down at the makeshift RAF base. Two of the escorting AE fighters landed soon afterwards while the other two patrolled overhead. Along with its speed, agility, range, high altitude, and stealth capabilities, the superlative AE fighter also had a VSTOL capability.

After a quick re-fuel of all aircraft, the Nimrod, still escorted by the fighters, headed into the interior of the Continental United States. The Nimrod followed a flight path a few hundred kilometers below the Canadian border.

The airspace of the continental United States and Canada was a veritable ghost yard. The Nimrod could not detect any airborne aircraft, friend or foe, with just one exception: the huge alien base ship in low geosynchronous orbit over Seattle for some reason. At the height of the war eight alien base ships had hovered over North America. No fighters came forth from the base ship to challenge the Nimrod and its escorts. Was this another sign of alien weakness? Though nothing was airborne, the Nimrod gathered in a variety of valuable electronic and other intelligence across large tracts of the United States and Canada.

The big aircraft went no closer than one thousand kilometers to the alien base ship. Though a reconnaissance aircraft, the Nimrod had come heavily armed. Before turning back the Nimrod and its escorts launched a long range missile (ELRAAM) attack on the base ship. Despite direct hits, the Drell ship survived indicating it still had some form of force field defense. Still, no retaliation came from the belly of the monstrosity.

Range was not a problem for the big Nimrod, but the magnificent AE fighters needed to return to Newfoundland and the Nimrod could not be left without fighter escort.

Ten kilometers outside New York Harbor, October 2025

At first the sound hardly registered, but it got progressively louder to the occupants of the old fishing boat. It was a sound they hadn't heard in months. The boat's occupants still couldn't see anything through the fog, though the helicopters had to be close.

Finally they saw them, five big machines flew almost directly above them and headed on over into the city. The downdrafts from the huge rotors almost sank the old boat. Anyone who knew their aircraft would have instantly recognized the helos. They were troop-carrying Super Merlins, but to the men on the boat they were just big helicopters. As the grey machines passed, the onlookers could see the fresh paint. There was no mistaking the words emblazoned on their sides: "Royal Navy." "Looks like the limeys are here," yelled someone.

"Thank God for that," said another occupant of the boat.

A few minutes later a second wave and then a third wave of the big helos headed over towards the city. There was the more distant sound of other helos, but they were farther away and could not be seen through the fog.

The real shock for the boat's occupants came just a little later. With the fog so thick, they didn't see the ship until it was quite close. It towered above them as it slowly moved on into New York Harbor. It was the big one itself, the super carrier HMS King George V, flagship of the Royal Navy. Although looking more than a little the worse for wear, it had somehow survived all the Drell attempts to destroy it.

The rest of the British fleet was a bit of a motley assortment. There were two of the magnificent Plymouth class laser destroyers and the new helicopter carrier HMS Exeter. However, in company with these fine ships were a couple of old Type forty-two destroyers and the one time ASW carrier, the Invincible, veteran of the Falklands war of forty-two years ago. Another veteran of that campaign, the assault ship Fearless, had also been dragged out of mothballs.

There had been just one alien attack on the British fleet as it came across the Atlantic. Suicidal, three of the compact ugly Drell fighters had come around in high stealth mode in a low orbit then descended at enormous speed. Every ship in the fleet fired on them. Pulse lasers from the KG5 and two Plymouth class destroyers finished them off. If that was the best the Drell could do, then they were definitely in trouble.

As paratroopers, royal marine commandoes, and Gurkha units were flown in by helicopter, the struggle for New York took on a new momentum. Soon these lightly armed shock troops were reinforced by regular army units from the assault ships in the harbour. Units from the Scots and Welsh Guards came and some heavy armor—Challenger Four main battle tanks—courtesy of the famous "desert rats." SAS and SBS already had pretty good information on the location of alien concentrations.

Down thousands of streets, ordinary New Yorkers, sometimes guided by SAS units, carried the fight to the aliens.

Where alien resistance was greatest, the elite British units were called in: the First and Second battalions of the Parachute Regiment, men of Forty and Forty Second Royal Marine Commandoes, and men from the Brigade of Gurkhas.

The aliens held on desperately to a disparate array of locations of no particular strategic significance: the New York Stock Exchange Building on Wall Street, Yankee Stadium, the ruins of the Chrysler and Empire State Buildings in Manhattan, and parts of Broadway among others. There were many strange scenes in the fighting for New York, perhaps none more so than force-field protected Challenger Four main battle tanks smashing their way into the Metropolitan Museum of Art.

Where possible, Royal Navy units in and outside of New York harbour provided gunfire and heavy duty laser support.

The fighting was unbelievably savage, beyond anything in past human experience, even Stalingrad. There at least men had fought men. Here it was alien versus man.

The Brits may have provided the organization, some vital weaponry, a modest number of troops, and some occasional heavy armor, but in the end it was the people of New York who took back their own city.

From the Super Merlin helicopter, Tittington took in a bird's eye view of New York. If the utter destruction surprised or alarmed him, he didn't show it. The big chopper landed back on the King George V. On the deck of the great ship, the Prime Minister looked across into the city.

He thought to himself. No one disputed that the Americans closely followed by the Chinese and the Indians had taken the brunt of the early Drell attacks. It was the military of these nations that had ripped the guts out of the aliens, but in doing so, they had all been defeated themselves.

"You'll have to remain here for the time being commander," he said "render them what assistance you can. Washington is next, when we are ready."

The Brits approach to wresting back most American cities was the same as they had used in New York. Basically they helped the Americans help themselves. In many cities the yanks had pretty much forced the aliens to a stalemate anyway. They just needed a little bit of help to break the deadlock.

Small numbers of Special Forces units would go in first and size up the situation. Existing resistance would be organized and given help and equipment. Modest numbers of elite troops, such as paratroopers and royal marine commandoes would then be brought in. Sometimes this was enough, but sometimes, as with New York and Washington, regular army units including armor had to be brought in. Where there was no other option, air support was provided.

The same approach was used for several of the big Canadian cities.

The Brits might have stayed a while and offered a bit of help, as they did in New York, but they didn't hang around. It was obvious the resourceful Americans would be on their feet very quickly, and there were demands elsewhere on the scarce British resources.

Australia had been helped, as had parts of Europe, but in the British sphere of influence India was going to be the real problem.

In their own sphere of influence, the island nation of Japan had attempted, with some degree of success, to do for China what the Brits had done for North America.

The last alien base ship above North America, the one above Seattle, had proven to be a toothless tiger. However, its protective force fields were still operational. In the end, a daring SAS raid on a still alien controlled B2 nuclear bomber base led to British acquisition of a number of still operational nuclear armed cruise missiles. Most of the American arsenal had either been disarmed by the aliens or used in the war.

The destruction by RAF bombers, using the recovered American cruise missiles, of the last alien base ship above North America was a largely symbolic act. However, its effect on morale almost everywhere went far beyond symbolism.

The Sky is the Wrong Color

Location: Unknown. Time: Unknown.

Earle looked out of the window of the modest passenger jet. Most people would not have picked it, but he could see the sky was different.

Asking to see the captain, he moved up towards the cockpit. At first the stewardess protested. "Tell him I know something is wrong," he said quietly and (hesitating) "tell him I'm the Equalizer."

Earle was ushered in immediately. The captain and his co-pilot looked greatly relieved.

"Do you have any idea what's happening sir?" said the captain (even then people still called the Equalizer sir). "We have no communications and most instrumentation has failed," continued the captain. "We are also using up fuel more rapidly than we should."

"We should land at the first opportunity," said Earle. "Mind if I take a look at your communications set up?"

Earle mucked about with the communications and some other instrumentation. After a couple of minutes he had most things working again. "How did you do that?" asked the co-pilot.

"Trade secret," laughed Earle.

Working again, the instrumentation indicated that the outside air was colder and thinner than it should be for the altitude. Communications seemed to be working, but there was no radio traffic at all, except for the oddest sounding radio beacon. There was one other thing. They should have over flown land about ten minutes ago, but there was nothing but sea below. The color of the sea seemed okay, at least to everyone except Earle, who knew better.

"It's a homing beacon of some sort," said Earle calmly. "I suggest we investigate it, probably our only option." The pilot changed course in the direction of the beacon. It was a minor course change, and the beacon was not far, assuming the instrumentation readings were true.

The color of the sky continued to change slowly. It became enough to concern a few of the passengers. Eventually a deputation came up to the cockpit. They were turned back with the promise that the captain would make an announcement.

"All right," said the pilot to Earle. "We've kept pretty calm, but if you have any idea at all what's going on here, now would be a good time to tell us."

"We have to tell the passengers something," added the co-pilot.

"Well, you're already sitting down," said Earle. "I'll give it to you straight," he continued. "Somehow or other we've entered an alternate reality."

The pilot and co-pilot just looked at him, like stunned mullets, neither saying anything. Finally the captain blurted out "If anyone else had said that, I would have laughed in their face."

"If you can't see it already," responded Earle "It'll become apparent soon enough after we land."

The passenger jet overflew the radio beacon's location. Below was a triangular shaped island, and a huge airport/transport facility seemed to be on it. The runways and airport buildings, if that's what they were, seemed to take up the whole island. The total area made JFK or Heathrow look like small regional facilities.

The captain's announcement came over the intercom. "This is Captain Gillespie, we are going to make a landing on the island facility below." The captain went on, "I know many of you are worried about our situation, but I can tell you that the Equalizer is on board this plane. Once we land and can assess the situation there, I'm sure he will know what to do."

Christine Lloyd the Chicago based neurosurgeon traveling with her daughter breathed a deep sigh of relief. So did pretty much everyone else on the plane. "We'll be all right," said someone. "The Equalizer never lets anyone down."

"Thank goodness for that," said someone else.

"Where to land?" asked the pilot looking at the confusing number of runways.

"Try that one," responded Earle smiling. "Just a hunch really." There were no other aircraft in the sky competing with them.

The plane landed and started to taxi in towards the monstrous building. It just got bigger and bigger as the plane approached.

The pilot looked at Earle. The Equalizer pointed to a part of the building. "Just a hunch again?" asked the pilot. Earle nodded.

Before the aircraft could reach the terminal, its engines failed completely. Some of the passengers became agitated. Earle steadied them. He went outside, noted the very cold and thin air, and then after rigging up a makeshift harness arrangement obtained from the cargo hold began to pull the plane towards the terminal. Several of the able bodied men on board had offered to help. Earle declined the offers primarily because of the outside conditions. Any ordinary person outside would need oxygen very quickly.

Earle continued to pull the jet. The thin air actually helped in some ways, and the strange surface of the runway seemed almost frictionless.

When the closest part of the colossal building was finally reached, Earle dropped the rigged up harness and looked for an entrance. If there was one, it was not immediately obvious.

He looked for touch, voice, other sound actuation of an entrance, and other possibilities. All to no avail. Finally he put the harness back on and towed the aircraft in a few more yards. Somehow that did the trick. Even after finding an entrance, Earle insisted that he go in alone before exposing anyone else to potential danger. He kept in touch with the plane through a short range two way radio. His commentary to the pilots was relayed to the rest of the passengers through the PA system.

Neither mobile nor satellite phones were working in this environment. Most passengers had already felt the need to satisfy themselves on this count and had made repeated attempts after the plane had landed.

When the passengers alighted, most of them needed oxygen masks to walk the fairly short distance into the building. As some of them looked upwards, the color of the sky continued to change getting more obviously weird by the moment. It had become a kind of purple orange with silvery streaks running through it. More than one passenger felt it was a portent of some kind.

The interior of the terminal building seemed, if anything, even more immense than was suggested from the outside. Each passenger brought with him or her two airline pre-packaged cold meals, a small bottle of water, and any hand luggage. There was no attempt to unload the suitcases in the cargo hold, and no one argued the point.

Much of the area inside the building consisted of huge travellator walkways and empty open spaces. On his first foray inside, Earle had located some kind of reasonable sized rest area, and this seemed as good a place as any for the passengers to sit down for a moment. The area contained a variety of different shaped chairs/lounges/beds, as if a variety of different physical forms was expected there. There were also touch activated spigots dispensing what seemed to be paste type foods and a variety of liquids. Everyone agreed to use up all of their pre-packaged meals and the drinks before even considering whatever came out of the spigots. If that became necessary, Earle said he would test them first.

It was strange how no one had voiced the matter that was on everyone's mind. A boy perhaps about fourteen finally gave voice to everyone's concern. "Where are all the people?" he asked. "This is the biggest place I've ever seen, but there's no one here." Earle told the passengers that even with his vastly heightened sensory capabilities, he could not sense a living thing anywhere in the huge complex. "What about robots?" the boy persisted, "or other artificial life forms such as androids or cyborgs?" His imagination had started to run away with him.

Earle didn't laugh. "Nothing currently operational" was his reply. "I would sense it if there were." These were not remarks that gave thc passengers any great comfort.

At the edge of the rest area was a crude computing facility. It contained only basic information, and Earle surmised that it was some sort of information booth. He was able to punch up some limited schematics of the building. Many areas on the schematics were simply marked as off limits, not by language but by an unmistakable pictorial symbol that cut across all language barriers. They would need to avoid these areas. Many other areas had no specific markings. The schematic also showed an area denoted by a pictorial symbol that Earle was unfamiliar with. It seemed very oblique and certainly did not transcend language barriers.

"We need to be able to access a better computing facility than this info booth," said Earle. "But we also all need to stay together." Earle asked the passengers if any among them had computing expertise. Several stepped forward including eleven year old Ju Hyeon Hong.

Fortunately it didn't take long to come across some kind of control room with better computing facilities than the booth. Although it was assuredly not any kind of master facility, Earle and Ju together were still able to extract the information they needed. The area denoted by the oblique symbol was a transit area for travelers from alternate realities who had come there inadvertently. It seemed this was an area where some alternate realities converged, and unintended visits by some occupants of those alternate realities were not uncommon. The homing beacon was meant to guide them in. They were then supposed to have been directed to land near and then enter the Alternate Reality Travelers Concourse. Something had gone wrong. They had received no directions from any source since the time of their arrival in this reality.

Earle and Ju managed to pull up some more detailed schematics. There were no more specific details on the off limits areas, but there was enough other information to help them get to the Alternate Reality Concourse.

There was something else. Earle quietly asked Ju to look away. He saw sufficiently enough to give him an insight into some of the other purposes of this terminal complex. These were less altruistic than helping lost persons return home. In fact, they made his stomach turn. Up until then Earle had been completely straight with the passengers, but this new information was in the need-to-know category. Definitely, very definitely none of the passengers needed to know about this.

Ju was more than a little scared as she looked up into Earle's eyes. "You will protect us Mr. Equalizer, won't you?" she said.

Earle looked unusually grim. "Yes, of course Hu," he said after an uncharacteristic pause.

Heading in the direction of the Alternate Reality Transit area, the passengers walked on through the colossal terminal complex. Where they could, they used the huge mile long travellator walkways, and other times they just walked. It became clear that rest areas, such as where they first stopped, were few and far between. *It was as if*, thought Earle, *large masses of people transited through these areas with little concern for any creature comfort*. Which of course he knew to be true.

Earle had concluded that the safest location for any alternate reality visitors to this place was the alternate reality concourse. If even that was safe in the present circumstances. Nobody in the group saw any reason to disagree with him. Somehow Earle knew that all of the group had to escape this place. While in this reality, their lives were inextricably linked. If one of them died or was lost, then none of them would return to their own reality. Not even Earle Gagne, the Equalizer.

There was no mistaking the alternate reality concourse, a facility that clearly catered for a vast array of different entities. By the time the group reached it, robotic mechanisms, which had been dormant in standby mode, were slowly becoming operational again. The sky outside was changing color almost continuously, getting weirder by the minute.

Everyone in the group felt a sense of desperate urgency.

Dotted about the huge concourse were what seemed to be evenly spaced computing facilities. Rushing to one such facility, which had the most human shape chairs near it, Earle, Hu, and another computer expert in the group, Mike Hammersmith, struggled to master the facility. It was more sophisticated than anything they had seen thus far in the complex.

Some of the group gathered about them, but the rest collapsed into what proved to be form fitting chairs, which might have accommodated almost any shape (perhaps humanoids were the last to have sat there). They looked out hopefully at the odd shaped crafts on the outside runway. Everyone hoped that a door of some kind might open or even hoped that one of the crafts might be controlled from the computing facility.

The small amount of food and water the group had brought into the complex was all but gone, and people were starting to experiment with the nearby spigots and their weirdly colored liquids and pastes.

Robotic devices were starting to appear at upper levels above the concourse. For what purpose none of the group knew, but all, except perhaps Earle, were extremely nervous.

Despite Earle's knowledge of advanced technologies and experience with alternate realities, it took the intuitive computer genius of Hu to make the breakthrough.

Smiling for the first time since they had entered the complex, Earle came over to the rest of the group. "I think we've worked it out," he said. "The computer doesn't activate a door to the outside runway or activate the aircraft."

"What does it do then?" piped up someone.

"We're pretty sure it's a portal to alternate realities," beamed Earle. "We just need to make sure we calibrate it to ours."

They did a trial run on someone's piece of hand baggage. Sure enough it disappeared, though no one could be sure exactly where.

Meanwhile some of the larger robotic devices were descending to the concourse level. At the same time several weird crafts appeared high above in the still changing sky. Descending straight down, they were clearly in a landing configuration. Earle sensed for the first time some mild telepathic probing on the group, though he couldn't tell where it emanated from or whether it was benevolent, malevolent, or just plain curious.

Perhaps there was really no reason to panic, but everyone was jumping out of their skins, and they were more than ready to take their chances on wherever the portal might lead.

So they jumped, or slid, or phased, or whatever else it is you do when you move from one reality to another.

As it turned out, they did arrive back on Earth, our Earth that is. One look at the sky was enough to tell Earle. Everyone else just knew from the fact that they had been deposited in the middle of Times Square, New York City. It could have been an alternate Times Square, of course, but take my word for it—there is only one Times Square!

Earle hadn't even gotten around to mentioning it, but he had been pretty confident. He knew the number of alternate realities were actually very finite. The alien computer appeared to have our reality very clearly in its memory ,and his programming instructions were very specific. Finally as a further precaution Earle and Hu had been able to program in a reference to the aircraft upon which they had arrived in the alternate reality.

Back on Earth, everybody just seemed to want to get away and go home, and the group quickly dispersed among the crowds of Times Square.

Not before Earle took his own quick head count though. To his dismay he counted five extra bodies among the group dispersing irretrievably among the crowds!

Return of the Protector

Somewhere in Northern Canada, Northern Hemisphere Summer, quite some years in the future

In all of her thirty-six years Kriz had never seen a storm like it. It had been raging for nearly two days and, if anything, seemed to be gaining in ferocity. The thunder was deafening to the point of physically damaging ear drums. The frequent lightning seemed to arc across the entire length of the sky. Sometimes it struck earthward with massive force. The rain had been very heavy and was increasing to torrential. Kriz had no way of knowing how widespread it was, but something told her it was big, very big. Perhaps even across all of NorAm.

Looking through the cabin window, she saw a man in the small clearing outside her modest cabin. *Surely nothing human should have to be out in this*, she thought. Partially opening her front door, she called for him to come in. Though he came at her call, he didn't seem to be in a hurry. *It's almost as if he's enjoying it*, she thought. As he almost reluctantly came in out of the storm, Kriz saw he was bigger than she had first thought: at least six and a half feet in the old measurements, maybe more and very powerfully built. He wore some sort of leggings, wrist bands, and a most impressive and ornate belt but was bare above the waist. Long blond almost golden hair dangled onto huge shoulders, and his chest seemed suggestive of great strength. He carried a large sack, which she had not noticed when she first hailed him. Kriz herself was a smidgen over six feet tall, and she had only once before met anyone taller. She felt almost dwarfed by this man.

He said something, but Kriz could not understand him. His voice was loud, almost guttural and the language seemed ancient Scando. He sounded how she imagined some of the

21

very ancient Vikings might have spoken. Kriz's small daughter Gab looked on fearfully as Kriz handed the man some crude toweling and offered him something hot to drink. As Kriz spoke some more the man adjusted his voice speaking more softly and in semi-understandable ancient Anglo Saxon.

Just then there was a fearful cracking sound above, and Kriz thought the whole world was about to collapse in on her little cabin. The small girl ran crying to her mother's side. Seeing the cause of the girl's and her mothers distress, the man seemed to make a very slight gesture, and the colossal raging storm outside ceased even more abruptly than it had begun. Kriz looked on with amazement "Did you do that?" she whispered.

"I don't know," said the man. "I think so, but I'm not sure." He was now managing to speak well enough in AmerEng, the native tongue of most of Earth's survivors.

Outside the sky was blue and totally cloudless, a normal warm summer's day in the temperate Northern Canada. As they settled down to a meal in the cabin, Kriz looked at the man for an explanation. He had been through a set of experiences that had nearly shattered his mind and was just then recovering a few fragments of his memory. He knew though that he had been absent from Earth for a very long time. The name Zunod came to his mind. He asked Kriz to relate her understanding of Earth's present position. She was happy enough to accommodate, sensing something of greatness in him, though she could not define it. Nodding at times, Zunod listened quietly to Kriz without interrupting. It seemed to him that man had finally done to himself what no would be extra-terrestrial invaders had ever succeeded in doing: man had finally laid his own planet bare. Earth was now seen as a backwater world. Only the lowliest alien scavengers, scum of the scum, came this way now. Earth was for the taking by any aliens who could reach it, but even they had almost stopped coming.

Towards the end of Kriz's discourse Gab came over towards Zunod as she seemed to warm to him. He noticed how pale and sickly she looked—a clear victim of the accumu-lated depredations these people had suffered. Kriz though was different, tall, attractive, and athletically built—Zunod pondered on this.

As Kriz finished, Zunod motioned for Gab to come over just a little further. Smiling, she obliged. For just a moment as Kriz watched, Zunod touched the child affectionately on the shoulder as if she were his own. A soft yellow, gentle healing glow appeared at Gab's shoulder and radiated to the rest of her small, frail body. The child screamed with delight. It was the sheer joy that can only be known by a person who has experienced constant pain all their lives and suddenly has been totally relieved of it. Kriz turned away for just a moment, wiping the tears away.

At that moment all three looked outside. There was no noise, but all sensed something. A woman seemed to come up from out of the very Earth itself. Of indeterminate age, she was beautiful in perhaps a slightly faded way. Still she had a great weariness suggestive of long suffering. Zunod seemed to know immediately who she was and moved to embrace her. He held her for what seemed to be quite a long time to Kriz who, though she knew it was unreasonable, ex-perienced a momentary jealousy. The woman moved away slightly but did not leave. The great weariness in her had gone as she smiled at Kriz. Kriz wondered if Zunod was some sort of healer.

After the embrace Zunod returned to the cabin and took a few items from his sack—a helmet, a studded vest, and something else. Kriz saw there was now a confidence about him that had been lacking—a purpose and certainty in his step.

"There are some things I have to do," said Zunod, "but my mother will see that you both have what you need."

Kriz was slow in her realization. She could not be blamed for this. It had been so long since the son of Odin had been among men that there was no record of his likeness. No per-son still living knew what form the ancient gods of Asgard had taken. The legend of the one time protector of Earth had persisted, but no one seriously believed that he still lived, much less that he would actually return one day.

As the mighty Thor took his leave, he called out to Kriz that he would be back. Twirling his hammer mjolnir about him, he soared skyward to view the condition of Earth for himself. Thor traversed all of the continents, the major islands, and the seas of Earth. He saw that all that Kriz had said was true and more. The relatively modest population of Earth now lived mainly in either very northerly or very southerly latitudes. The equatorial regions of Earth were far too hot for human habitation. The continental part of the great southern land, once known as Australia, was no longer inhabited by humans. Only the spirits of ancient warriors from the dreamtime watched over that land. Less than a hundred indigenous persons lived on in the roasting heat of the island of Tasmania. The population of the continental United States was very small, restricted to what had formerly been very cold areas.

At some places, formerly of significance, Thor stopped and descended. Among them were the crumbling ruins of a semi submerged place, which had once been the greatest city Earth had ever known—New York City. Now no one at all lived there.

Though his mother had imprinted all of this in his mind, the son of Odin had needed to see it all for himself.

Thor made one final stop before returning to Northern Canada. At the rooftop of the world—Mount Everest. Structurally the great Himalayas mountain range was unchanged but the snow and ice that should have been in abundance were conspicuous by their absence.

On Everest Thor took a moment for reflection. His mind turned back to when the Living Tribunal had come, and he had answered the call to arms. There had been no choice really. As the most powerful God in all of the Multiverse's pantheons, his participation had been essential. Later all of Earth's pantheons, including all of Asgard, were drawn into the conflict. Very few of the great powers of the Multiverse, Gods, abstract beings, or other cosmic entities had survived. In some ways this had led to a ceding of authority to the middle level powers of the Multiverse—both individual entities and star spanning empires. The final battle for existence had occurred at the "All Place." A place where all the different realities converge. In the end and simply put, victory could not have been achieved without the son of Odin.

Thus, what had happened to Earth had to be seen in context. Unfortunately mortal man's time frame is quite different from that of the Gods or the cosmic powers. A human analogy might be the man who saves his country but fails to save his family.

Thor then summoned forth the elements bidding them to play their part in the long healing process of Earth. Immediately gentle rains began falling where it was most needed across vast areas of the dry Earth. Caressing the deserts, steppes, and other areas, the rain began the first step in readying them for when men might return.

Thor made two deviations on his flight back to Canada: one planned and one unplanned. First he flew to Earth end of the rainbow-bridge dimensional link to Asgard. He could see Asgard City still where it should be. Thor knew there should be no one in Asgard City. The life forces of all Asgardians without exception had participated in the final battle for the Multiverse. The Odin son could sense no life forces whatever within the City. However, he could not bring himself to go into the City at this time—to walk among the long empty halls and rooms and courtyards. He would come back another time.

The second detour was unplanned but necessary. Thor had sensed the approach of an alien scavenger fleet. He made short work of them by smashing most of their starships but allowing the survivors to return in two vessels. It enabled him to vent some frustrations. More importantly it provided a clear message to other potential intruders that Earth was once again under his protection. The word would not take long to get around.

Thor returned to Kriz and little Gab. He knew now the reason why Kriz was so athletic and vital in a world where the few survivors were usually the opposite. Gaea had whispered it to him during their embrace. Though even Kriz did not know it—she was the embodiment of the future of humanity in human form. Thor saw that already all manner of vegetables overflowed from Kriz's garden and well laden fruit trees were in abundance. He knew that Gaea had done much the same for all other people that still dwelled upon Earth. Along with the rains he had started, it was a small beginning, and he and Gaea had much to do.

He looked at Kriz and smiled taking her in his arms as little Gab held on to his knee. If Kriz was in truth the living embodiment of the future of humanity, then from where he was standing that future looked pretty good.

The Trouble with Suez

The Mediterranean Sea, October 1956

"Look's like they mean business," shouted Gary Bowers to his co-pilot Chuck Teager as their two seater version of the normally one seater U2 reconnaissance plane flew at just over seventy thousand feet above the Mediterranean Sea.

Far below them a large fleet of British and French warships including aircraft carriers was steaming through the Eastern Mediterranean. Their destination was unknown, but the Americans knew it had to be the Suez Canal.

"Don't look now but we've got company," said Gary. At this height American U2 pilots would expect to have the skies to themselves, but sailing almost serenely into view were two RAF English Electric Lightning interceptors. They made no attempt at communication.

"Thought we'd be safe at this height," said Chuck, matter of factly.

Something not right here, thought Gary. *As far as I know the Lightning isn't any where near operational yet.* The next moment one of the RAF fighters fired a short range air-to-air missile across the bow of the U2; it exploded only just at a safe distance.

"What the hell," yelled Gary. "Since when does the RAF fire on U.S. military aircraft, and whatever happened to normal NATO communication channels?"

"NATO?" asked Chuck. "What's that?" Gary took a quick worried side ways look at his co-pilot but was too busy to pursue the matter.

"We can't stay here," said Chuck. "As far as I know, those screamers can do mach two or more." Gary went to communicate with the Lightning pilots, but Chuck signaled it would be a waste. The U2 peeled well away from the naval vessels below although the Lightnings stayed with them for a while.

27

"I guess Harris can expect a phone call from Ike on this," said Chuck. "Not that bomber will take any notice."

"Harris?" asked Gary.

"Arthur Harris—the British Prime Minister. Not keeping up on politics Gary?" laughed Chuck.

"So whatever happened to Anthony Eden," asked Gary nonchalantly.

"Never heard of him," said Chuck.

Pilot and co-pilot went quiet after that exchange. Gary was still stunned by the RAF firing on them, but he was even more concerned and puzzled by his co-pilot's remarks. He decided to say as little as possible for the rest of the flight. However, towards the end of the flight he ventured a comment "Arthur Harris—as in Bomber Harris, head of Bomber Command in World War Two?"

"The one and only," replied Chuck. Gary's face went quite white. Thoughts of Cologne, Hamburg, Berlin, and most particularly Dresden went through his mind.

"Of course the Sixth Fleet would have been following the Brit Fleet a lot more closely, but after the Vulcan over flight, we backed off—but you know all this," rambled Chuck. Gary hadn't a clue what Chuck was talking about. "Damn Limeys over flew the Sixth Fleet with about forty Vulcan Bombers with all their latest electronic jamming in operation—completely threw out the Fleet's communications." As far as Gary knew, the RAF had about one prototype Vulcan Bomber doing the rounds—it would be a good bomber one day!

After arrival back at base and during some time off, Gary did quite a bit of checking up and more than a little reading on current events and recent history. Mostly things seemed as they should be—the airbase and the people all seemed about the same.

Gary confirmed that Arthur Harris was indeed the Prime Minister of Great Britain, and that the RAF did apparently have fairly large numbers of operational English Electric Lightning fighters and Vulcan jet bombers.

A little closer attention to recent historical events found some of the details to be quite different from Gary's recollection. The grand alliance of World War Two had, as he remembered, held up for most of the war. However, things took a twist in March 1945 that weren't in any history books that he'd read before.

British and American commanders had disagreed over how to deal with Berlin. Contrary to Gary's recollection Churchill, Brooke, and Montgomery had not knuckled under to the Americans and Montgomery's twenty-first Army Group had gone ahead and beaten the Russians into the city. Then RAF Bomber Command chief Arthur Harris had even led the way organizing a fifteen hundred heavy bomber raid just in front of the advancing Russians. It was said to be assisting them, but in fact it was Churchill and Harris's clear warning for the Russians not to interfere in Berlin. Harris even arranged for follow up RAF jet fighter and jet bomber raids. Gloster Meteors and Canberra Bombers. *Canberra jet bombers*, thought Gary. *the Brits may have had Meteor fighters at the end of the war but the Canberra Bomber came later on.*

Gary read how British and American relations were never the same after this, and the post war world had developed as a tri-polar, rather than the bi-polar one that he knew with bitter rivalries, between the United States, Britain, and Russia continuing to the present day.

Taking his head out of the books, Gary Bowers realized that the Suez "crisis" had continued to unfold. British, French, and Israeli intentions becoming clear with the occupation of the Suez Canal.

Airmen at Gary Bower's USAAF base in Italy were discussing the matter in the mess. "Ike is furious," said someone, "but apparently Harris isn't even taking calls from him."

"Surely all we have to do is pull the financial plug on the British," said Gary. "There'll be a run on the pound and Eden, sorry, Harris will have no choice other than to pull the troops out. Also the Russians will have none of it."

"Where the hell have you been," said someone else. "Khrushchev has been posturing and blustering about Soviet armored columns for days now, and the Brits aren't taking a blind bit of notice."

"As to the financial side—the Brits have suspended all trading in the pound sterling," volunteered another airman. "And the pound is a floating currency in conjunction with other major European currencies—we can't hurt them quickly enough."

Gary followed events in the media over the next few days. For all his anger Eisenhower seemed powerless, but eventually Khrushchev made good on his threat, and Soviet armored columns rumbled towards Suez. Somewhere around that time Harris, fed up with both Khrushchev and Eisenhower, decided to call the Soviet leader's bluff. The two hundred V Bombers of RAF Bomber Command, loaded with a combination of free fall and blue steel short stand-off nuclear bombs, were put on alert. Eventually as the Soviet columns rolled out over the Sinai Peninsula, Harris's bombers were in the air.

By the time Khrushchev, in his brinkmanship, called off his armor, it was too late; the RAF had passed the point of no return. One thing was certain, Harris was not going to blink first. RAF free fall and stand-off nuclear weapons began falling on Kiev, Kursk, Smolensk, Moscow, Leningrad, Volgograd, and many other Russian cities.

Gary Bowers, U2 pilot in the United States Air Force woke up sweating profusely the next day. It must have all been just a bad dream—what other explanation was there for it all. Greatly relieved he went down to the mess hall just in time to witness the first television pictures of the Russian atomic attack on London.

All Father

Thousands of millions of light-years from Earth there exists the largest and oldest black hole in our Universe. In itself there is nothing remarkable about this. However, the same black hole exists in all the different dimensions of our Multiverse. It is the only naturally occurring multi-dimensional black hole in existence.

It is said that its gravitational pull is so immense that, when close, only the great powers of our Multiverse can escape it. For untold ages unfortunate worlds, star fleets, and individual starships approaching too close, from whatever dimension, have been sucked into the gravitational well, never to be seen again. It is said that if they could survive those intense gravitational pressures in anyway at all, they would be spewed out of our Multiverse into the timeless, limitless void that exists beyond. Sometimes spoken of as the ethereal sea. The ever watchful great powers are used to things going into the black hole. They are not used to anything coming back out.

Hlidskialf in the Asgardian plane of existence

Standing in the elevated place of Hlidskialf and dressed in full battle armor, great Odin Lord of the Norse Gods of Asgard looked into the time stream to view the alternate near futures. They were all exactly the same and all equally bleak. Each showed a steady flow of awesomely powerful entities streaming from the black hole into every single dimension of our Universe. *It is everyone and everything that ever posed a threat to the Multiverse and was eventually destroyed,* thought Odin.

"How is it that these dark powers can exist again father?" asked Odin's son the legendary Thor, God of Thunder, "after they were so completely destroyed?"

"They have not been taken from the time stream mighty Thor," responded Odin. "Rather it seems that they have been re-created, all of them, down to the minutest detail by that which is the power beyond the power and now exists only in the timeless, endless void of the ethereal sea."

"Then let us all hope that he regains his sanity," finished Thor.

Suddenly and totally without warning Asgard, home of the Norse gods, was almost overwhelmed by an energy surge beyond anything it had heretofore known.

In viewing events from Hlidskialf, Allfather Odin had thought he was viewing near future merging alternatives. He had thought that there was still some small element of time in which he could prepare for the defense of Earth and Asgard. This was not so, as the near future alternatives became the moment.

Odin gathered his great shield the legendary Odin Shield and threw it out amidst the fray. While it appears as just a normal Asgardian shield, the Odin Shield can assume almost any size and can act as a force field protection for a city, a continent, or even an entire planet if needed. Created long ago by Odin and the ancient Brell civilisation working together, it immediately cocooned all Asgard from the indescribable power of the attack.

Any one of these several threats confronting Asgard had been powerful enough to threaten all of existence. The pressure on the Odin Shield was unbearable and totally unrelenting, and the shield began to heave and buckle.

As Odin, Thor and all of the Asgardian Gods prepared for battle the onslaught against them briefly ceased.

The nature of the threat left great Odin with no option other than to draw on the most ancient spell in all of Asgardian cosmology, one that had never been used and therefore had never been tested in the field. Notwithstanding that, it was in actual fact the most powerful mystical spell in all of existence. It was so powerful that it could be used once and once only. As Odin stated the short incantation and gestured as if it were a piece of magic that he used daily, it worked with singular efficiency. In less time than a single beat of a butterfly's wings, all those forces of evil ranging once again against Asgard and indeed all of the Multiverse were momentarily frozen in time.

"We have only one choice," said Odin, "in the mere moments before our enemies overcome the great spell."

"You must go father," said the mighty Thor "there is no one else really. You must go and attempt to reason with the power that is beyond all powers, he who is above us all."

Odin hovered at the edge of the huge multi-dimensional black hole's massive gravitational pull. The mighty Thor accompanied him. "You must remain here my son," said the Allfather. "If I fail, you are our only hope." With that Odin allowed himself to be drawn into the largest naturally occurring gravitational well in existence. For the slightest moment he lingered at the core of the black hole then chose not to resist the inevitable forces that thrust him out beyond our Multiverse into the timeless, limitless void beyond.

Every one of the different Universes that go to make up our Multiverse is limited in some way or other, whether it be by curvature in a higher dimension or some other mechanism. Thus in reaching the edge of a Universe, one finds oneself come in at the opposite extremity or sometimes moving into another dimension.

This is not so for the limitless void or ethereal sea beyond. There one could travel the equivalent of trillions of light years and not make any impression on what is truly, not just practically, infinite. In other words, one could travel all that distance and effectively go nowhere at all. Odin saw that there was nothing in the void—well almost nothing. He sensed the irradiated power of that which is beyond the beyond, the power beyond the power. The source of the irradiated power was inconceivably distant. So much so that Odin would need to use not inconsiderable reserves to teleport that distance. He would have to in a place where there were clearly no additional wells or reserves of power that he could draw on other than his own heavily depleted personal reserves. *It is as if having set a clockwork Newtonian Multiverse in operation, he who is above us all decided to retreat from all further participation*, thought Odin.

At not inconsiderable effort Odin teleported a distance beyond even his imagination. At his destination he found a large throne room strangely like his own. Except of course, someone else was seated upon the throne. No doubt the semi familiar environment was for Odin's benefit. *I am one of the great powers of the Multiverse*, thought Odin, *but here in this place that means exactly nothing*. Unthinkably far beyond any form of help, his energy reserves depleted for the moment, and far beyond access to other reserves, Odin realized he could almost certainly be struck down on the barest whim of the occupant of the throne. In his weakened state, Odin was not certain that he could even teleport back the inconceivable distance to the void side of the multi-dimensional black hole under his own power.

"Lord," said Odin both in physical speech (for all its remoteness this was still a physical place rather than some abstraction) and telepathically. "What are you doing to us?"

The occupant of the Throne arose. He reminded Odin somewhat of a more majestic version of his own father. Again presumably a comfort thing.

The entity hesitated. "Odin, _____ I have been lonely."

Odin's first fleeting thought was that he who was the power beyond the power had gone mad, at least in terms of Odin's frame of reference, but as they talked at the greatest length, Odin saw that this was not so. Time meant absolutely nothing in this place. When Odin returned to the Multiverse, one hundred billion years might have elapsed or no time at all.

"Come again Allfather," said he who is above us all.

Odin teleported with ease to the ethereal sea side of the multi-dimensional black hole and via that he again entered our Multiverse. He had never felt so well, so thoroughly refreshed, even as a child. Thor awaited him at the edge of the gravitational well. To Thor's perception Odin had simply entered and immediately returned from the black hole. Though in that instant Thor knew that the threat against the Multiverse had simply ceased to exist.

Odin related the essence of events but nothing of his discussion with The One Above All. Much of that was not something he could or would share with anyone. "It would be best then not to leave it so long before someone visits him again," said Thor almost smiling.

"Others were remiss in this," said Odin.

"He who is above us all would be content with a visit every few billion years," finished Allfather Odin also almost smiling.

The Battle of London

The roaming youthpak was larger than anything ever seen in what was left of England and was still growing.

It seemed to begin as just a malicious nuisance made by a few ferals, but as it grew, the realization dawned that the juggernaut would be very hard to stop. Small gangs, and lone youth were joining the pak just for the ride.

The residual "authorities," such as they were, were almost powerless in the face of such large numbers of well armed miscreants.

The best the authorities could manage was to "divert" the gathering storm from any still populated areas with crude aerial bombing. This was from a motley assortment of small unmanned surveillers and a few piloted rotaries. Most of which were shot down. Manned fixed wing aircrafts were a luxury of the past.

The youth bore all manner of arms. A select few (those seemingly in control) had relatively modern lasrifles. A few more had the ancient but venerable very high rate of fire (VHRF) machine rifles. A number of exo-skeletons were spread among the pak. Usually these had been broken into parts, but the innovative ferals had still been able to keep them operational. Improvised explosive devices (IED's) of many different types were plentiful among the youth. There was also a sprinkling of low powered energy prods and energy knuckledusters and huge numbers of the blinding, irritant laspens. The youth had other more makeshift but no less dangerous weaponry, a testament to their ingenuity.

"What I wouldn't give for one left over tactical nuke," remarked one of the ever diminishing law enforcers. But of course the "nukes" had long since either been scrapped or actually used once control of them came down to City Councils. That the "authorities" would use them if they had been available was not in doubt.

The ever diminishing Greater London City Council (GLCC) and their small police arm represented the main residual semblance of authority in all of Southern England.

The youthpak had been assembling and moving in a largely destroyed and deserted part of the metropolis. However, their movements had brought them relatively close to the Croydon Neighborhood Watch Area (CNWA). If the youth started to move into this area, it would be a bloodbath even by the standards of this very bloody time.

Although CNWA had definitely seen better days it was still the best equipped Neighborhood Watch Area in England. Part day operational force fields for some of the less damaged housing and still standing public buildings, still operational android internal security, and a piloted light helo were a few of the things at their command. Most of all though, they had a good stock of the Model 239 Just Over The Horizon (JOTH) long range sniper rifles. The last military ordinance made before the Government factories closed. All were in good working order. More than this, CNWA had some older ex-military who really knew how to use them. Rumor had it CNWA even had a few ex-SAS on board. Although the troopers were getting a bit long in the tooth.

There were no Government or national armed forces anymore. Not anywhere in Europe leastways.

Occasionally the GLCC and CNWA might team up, like now with the youthpak threat, and that was as good as it got.

The GLCC aerial bombing, such as it was, had done nothing to alter the loose general direction of the rolling, roiling mass of youth, and several of the pilotless drones had been destroyed. Drones they couldn't afford to lose.

From their high watch towers at the edge of the neighborhood area the CNWA, snipes stood ready. As it came into snipe range just below the horizon and before they could possibly respond, the youthpak was hit with volleys of deadly accurate fire. Scores of them fell, but it only seemed to simply galvanize them. If anything, it sped up their approach to the CNWA. From the vantage point of the towers, the snipes saw evidence of a disciplined and efficient elite operating within the seething mass of youth. These leaders were happy to use the mass as a shield.

Once in range the youthpak leaders, that is those with the lasrifles, concentrated their fire on one watchtower at a time. Eventually the towers also came into range of the nasty little laspens held by quite a few of the youth. By then the snipes had to withdraw from the remaining watch towers to prepared positions among buildings guarding the approaches to the CNWA.

The snipes were now using the JOTH sniper rifles in a less conventional role, remaining behind cover and using a slight curvature of the projectiles.

The youth took heavy losses with the CNWA snipes trying to target their suddenly very wary leadership.

Perhaps it was a lack of confidence in their defenses or more likely a lack of intestinal fortitude but, at a crucial point in the battle, the CNWA coordinators decided to skip town. They left in three ancient internal combustion transportation devices powered by bio-fuels. The older coordinators remembered that these used to be called cars. Running alongside the slow moving transporters went some of the best of the CNWA's ageing ex-special forces troopers, and with them went any remaining chances of holding out against the youthpak.

After that extemporized withdrawal, the youthpak, still taking losses from snipefire, lasfire, and just plain ordinary fire, started to overrun parts of the neighborhood watch area.

Not unreasonably the youth picked up any weapons of value that their fleeing adversaries may have left.

Earle Gagne, perhaps the best and certainly the youngest of the ageing ex-SAS troopers, had chosen not to go with his masters in their ignominious retreat. Instead, he held out in one of the force field protected buildings. Raging feral, rather than merely menacing, some of the youth surrounded the nearest force field protected buildings. They were confident in the knowledge that the force bubbles could not be maintained for long and for even less time when they were under lasfire.

Some of the force bubble protected buildings had basements, sub-basements, and short escape corridors surfacing in unlikely locations. Earle and fellow snipe and ex-SAS trooper "Aussie Joss" Williams, a short muscular brunette of indeterminate age, decided to utilize the escape route. The tunnel from this particular building was one of the longest in the CNWA and surfaced under a particularly large pile of rubble away from the youth.

Earle and Joss could have headed off almost anywhere to get well away from the exultant youthpak. Instead they chose to head for the GLCC headquarters just north of the old city centre of London.

It was a pretty fair bet that after the pak finished up in the CNWA, that's where its controllers would seek to direct it. The GLCC was the only remaining obstacle to the pak's total dominance of southern England.

Earle refused to think about the possible fate of the inhabitants of the CNWA and their betrayal by the watch coordinators. He simply blanked this out from his mind. At least for the moment. Though he did not dismiss the possibility of revenge on both youthpak and watch coordinators.

The duo moved cautiously through the urban wasteland in their short trip up from Croydon to what, an eternity ago, had been the heart of empire. The superlative JOTH sniper rifles were slung on their backs, while they held hand weaponry more suited to close quarter urban fighting.

They encountered a few straggling youth along the way but went largely unchallenged. In small numbers the stragglers were not nearly as feral as in the Pak. Perhaps just a few of the youth, the more reasonable among them, were becoming revolted by it all.

From some of the still standing buildings grim faces appeared through glassless, wood boarded windows. Earle knew these dwellings for what they were. Unprotected houses of ill repute. The oldest profession of all still flourished. Earle marveled that they stayed on though. When the youthpak came through, as inevitably it would, he didn't give much for their chances.

Overhead came the occasional pilotless drone and the even less than occasional piloted rotary or helo as they used to be called. Very soon afterwards came the exploding sound of free falling incendiaries. More often than not the drones or rotors did not return. Earle fervently hoped that the GLCC had something more up their sleeve than this.

As Earle and Joss moved through it, the city centre of London, nowadays almost total rubble, was deathly quiet. If anyone was about, they didn't show it.

Only when they moved just north of the city did they encounter a small GLCC police "snatch unit" which escorted them the short distance to GLCC HQ. From a distance that monolithic edifice still looked imposing. The former HQ of the legendary and semi-mystic EMIFIVE. Still the closer they got, the less formidable the huge structure seemed. Former control posts, check points, and defensive barriers were in an advanced state of disrepair and unmanned. The once mighty emergency force shields, designed to protect against a direct nuclear strike, were a mere shadow of their former selves.

Earle noticed small groups of police deployed in defensive positions on the approaches to the building. Though well equipped, they seemed frighteningly small in number. Most of them did not even seem to be that well concealed. Earle was totally dismayed.

On entry to the GLCC, Earle was taken to the head of that much diminished organization a now elderly man who was known to him. A "Jimmy" Bond sometimes referred to as 007 for originally humorous reasons that were now lost in obscurity. No doubt something to do with the former occupiers of the building.

Even as Earle sat down with Jimmy, on the highly protected top floor of the GLCC, the first long range shots came in from over the horizon courtesy of captured JOTH sniper rifles.

"Things are looking pretty bad Earle," said Jimmy, "but then I don't need to tell you that."

"A small tactical nuke might be handy right about now," remarked Earle. "A shame the Council used them up north years ago."

The head of the GLCC looked very strangely at Earle. "There is a small matter that I would like your opinion on."

As they entered the sub basement Earle took a look at the few still operational 3D overview cams. The police units protecting the approaches to the GLCC were now under heavy pressure and starting to fall back into the building which itself was taking on increasing fire. For the moment the building's light force shields, only operational at the lower levels and separately at the very top level, were holding.

Earle looked on with more than casual surprise. Before him was the smallest nuclear fusion reactor he had ever seen. "Still operational," said Jimmy Bond. "Possibly the last one anywhere in the world." Bond continued in a quieter tone, "they tell me you know how to overload one of these things?"

Above ground it seemed that the bulk of the remaining youthpak was on the approach to the GLCC edifice. The rate of lasrifle, JOTH projectile, VHRF machine rifle, and even laspen fire steadily increased. At the base of the building youth under considerable police fire were affixing and linking a cunningly macabre array of Improvised Explosive Devices.

Youth casualties were considerable, but they came on in a fashion reminiscent of the Chinese or Russian armies hundreds of years before them. They came on in a world where the population was so diminished, Earle wondered where so many youth could have come from. Of course, there were no longer any reliable population estimates. Still it seemed to Earle there must be many more people subsisting in the nooks, crannies, basements, and cellars of the sprawling urban rubble than anyone had thought possible. Youth had also come in from outlying areas of the former capital and other parts of Southern England.

When the small fusion reactor exploded it was less effective than the GLCC chief had hoped. Still, at that stage many of the youth were milling triumphantly throughout all levels of the building. They intended to ransack it totally before destroying it with the IED's. The explosion from the fusion reactor actually set off the crude and even the not so crude IED's. In hardly anytime at all the structure collapsed.

Not all the youth were in the building, and some within escaped its collapse. Still the GLCC police having withdrawn via basement tunnels were ready for the survivors.

Mercifully it was over quickly.

There was understandable euphoria among the defending GLCC police. Many of them knew with utter disgust what had happened to the inhabitants of the Croydon Neighborhood Watch Area.

In time all that evaporated. In a world where there had seemed to be so few survivors of any age, a surprising number of its youth had come forth out of the urban ruins only to perish. Perhaps this society was better off without the hard core of ferals that had started the pak, but there were many among them that were just swept up by the moment

It was a loss this already vastly diminished, scarcely recognizable society, would never recover from.

What is any society without its youth?

The Judgment

Our Solar System, Several Millennia in the future

The energy configuration had traveled far and at great speed. It was crossing galactic systems in mere hours as humankind once measured time. By its own assessment the configuration had been gone hardly any time at all. Though others with a different frame of reference would have measured its absence in millennia.

Throughout its journey the configuration was constantly absorbing vast amounts of data from the galaxies it passed through. As its journey progressed, a sense of urgency and even of foreboding came over it: thought patterns it had no longer considered itself capable of having. The entity increased its speed to the point where it was traversing Galaxies in mere minutes. Finally its journey came to an end.

As it moved into the star system of humankind, the configuration already knew what would greet it. Earth, the cradle of human civilisation, was no more. Where the small blue green world had once been there existed only swirling debris. Nor was the destruction in the Sol system confined to Earth. Earth's moon had also been destroyed as had man's one frail and disappointing attempt at inter-planetary exploration—the Martian colony. Evidence of the battle was widespread. The advanced technology of Earth's armed forces had joined with the mystical/magical powers of the ancient Norse gods.

The configuration searched for evidence of the author(s) of Earth's destruction. It seemed likely that the events were the result of a Celestial judgment upon mankind. To confirm this suspicion the configuration looked back into the time stream and silently witnessed the last moments of mankind. A quiet anger and sadness arose within it in equal measure. The Celestial host was indeed responsible, but Earth had not gone quietly. The Celestial judgment and its subsequent execution had been carried out with one notable absentee among Earth's defenders. Would the Celestials have still attempted this if he had been present in his past form? It was a moot point.

Where once had been the legendary inter-dimensional link from Earth to the Norse Gods of Asgard, the magnificent rainbow bridge, stood an ugly sore. A permanent gaping hole in the dimensional barrier between Earth and Asgard. Barely recognizable figures scurried back and forth through the hole and between Asgard and the debris that was once Earth. The new overlords of Asgard had allowed it to deteriorate beyond all recognition.

Is this it then? thought the configuration. *Is this how it all ends, for humanity, for the Norse gods and for all who held Earth dear? Judged unsuitable, all that men and Gods had aspired to, crushed by little more than a Celestial whim.*

The anger welled within it/him, and it/he made no attempt to suppress that anger. His first act was to remove all the parasites from Asgard and the Sol environs, both the new overlords and their sycophantic underlings. He did not much care where he sent them as long as it was far away. The other side of the Universe would be enough.

The energy configuration then scoured the remains of the battle. Mostly there were just fragments left of the most durable weapons that Earth's defenders had utilized. Anything else would have been vaporized in the conflict. Nearing the end of the search, impossibly, unbelievably, he came across that which he knew had prompted the search. There it lay—darkened, pitted and fractured, but essentially whole. One of the very greatest weapons in the whole history of the Multiverse. Feared by God, man, and cosmic entity alike—the great hammer of Thor, God of Thunder. Gentle fingers of energy passed over the hammer repairing it, making it whole again. Of the few recognizable remnants of artifacts and weapons to be found, this was the only one that the energy configuration initially restored.

But where, thought the configuration. *Where are the Norse Gods? Where is the mighty Thor?* The energy configuration's brief look back into the time stream had not provided it/him with a clear answer to this question. *It was time*, thought the energy configuration, *to devolve from his present form back to that which he once was.* In truth he wasn't quite sure if such an act of devolution was possible anymore. Still it must at least be attempted and so with not inconsiderable effort that which had once been was so again. The regal figure surveyed the destruction again, but this time in his physical Godly form, that of Odin the Almighty, the former Lord of Asgard and onetime Allfather to an entire race of gods. And with this devolution the Universe, nay the Multiverse itself, somehow seemed to breathe just a little easier.

Even before he left us for places beyond our comprehension, Odin was one of the great powers of the Multiverse. Now he had returned from a place beyond and was even more of a force to be reckoned with.

That which had again become Odin, re-created Asgard in all its former glory with the exception that not a single living God stood within it. Then without so much as taking a breath, that which was again Odin recreated Earth. It was an Earth as it had been in the early days of man—pure and unpolluted. Though again and for the nonce, not so much as one single living person dwelled thereon. Earth's moon was restored in the same breath. Finally Odin repaired the gaping inter-dimensional breach between Earth and Asgard. The once Allfather considered drawing together the remnants of the destroyed artifacts and weapons used in Earth's defense and creating a monument to the events of the past. But this was too morbid and hardly appropriate. Events had not yet fully run their course.

Were the architects of Earth's destruction now witnessing his return? Might they not choose to intervene again? Daring to challenge even him? What was their protocol if a world upon which they had passed and executed judgment was subsequently restored by another power? Odin looked up; there were more pressing considerations—the Celestials could wait—but there would come a reckoning!

After recreating both Asgard and Earth, Odin decided to again look back into the time stream and view the end of mankind for indications as to the fate of the Gods. He watched and watched again the destruction of Earth. Odin considered going back in time not to alter past events, but to be there as they actually occurred and to render moral judgment on the Celestials at that time. This moral judgment would be followed by an actual physical judgment in the present day. He decided against this course of action. He had already learned enough from viewing the time stream to hold some hope in his heart.

The former Lord of Asgard approached the unharmed planet Venus. There he sought out a former lover. Jord or Gaea the Earth Mother, the very embodiment of the Earth. It was impossible to imagine Odin's delight when he was able to gently escort the mother of mighty Thor back to Earth. The Earth mother was the first sentient entity to take up residence on the recreated Earth. It could not possibly have been more appropriate. *There is yet hope*, thought Odin.

In viewing the past Odin had seen that mere moments before Earth's destruction it had been uninhabited. In a truly prodigious feat, the mighty Thor had inter-dimensionally teleported not only all humanity but all living things upon Earth to a pre-planned destination—a distant pocket dimension.

Odin was initially unable to locate humanity. In his efforts to protect mankind from the Celestials, Thor had chosen well. Asgard's former Lord attempted to filter out all relevant distractions and using his ability to listen inter-dimensionally, he focused on humanity. From a most distant and inaccessible pocket dimension he heard their faint cries. Thor's spell had begun to wear off, and humankind was awakening in the crowded location where they had been transported. Odin recreated all of the trappings of civilisation on Earth (buildings, vehicles, infrastructure, etc.) as they had been immediately before the Celestial attack, and then he teleported all of humanity and all other living things of Earth back to their home.

Odin's acts of creation dwarfed the acts that led to the original destruction of Earth. Ultimately it is always much easier to destroy than to create.

Mere moments after humanity's return to Earth, the enigmatic Celestials appeared at a distance thousands of kilometers from Earth. They took no overt action. They were simply there, impassive, unmoving, and intimidating. Odin ignored this for a time, though it was an irritation to him. It was as if Odin had somehow crossed over a line in the sand that the Celestials had drawn. Returning humanity, who had been judged unworthy, to a recreated verdant Earth was presumably that act.

As the Celestials confronted him, Odin reverted back to what had become his true form, the massive energy configuration. He protectively enveloped all of Earth and in this task was enjoined unexpectedly by others of his kind—four other energy configurations.

What price were the Celestial host prepared to pay to ensure that their original judgment upon humankind was enforced? Just possibly, against Odin alone as a physical God or even energy form they might have triumphed. Up against Odin and four others of his kind they were outmatched and they knew it.

Now might have been the time for great Odin to carry out an unmistakable demonstration of power, something the Celestials could not possibly misconstrue. As a physical God he might have been tempted, but as an energy configuration from a higher plane of existence he was above this.

Odin gave the Celestials a very clear picture of the future of humankind, which totally contradicted the basis for their earlier judgment. It showed man overcoming all his current problems and ascending to a greatness among the stars, a greatness that would one day eclipse even the Celestials. As they witnessed this glimpse of the future of mankind, the Celestials knew it to be so.

Thus did it end. In a precedent unknown since times aborning, a Celestial's judgment had been successfully reversed. What happened today would live on in stories to be passed down for all time.

Also just as long as there were men upon Earth and Gods in Asgard, Odin knew that the Celestials would not come this way again.

The Day Nobody Died

No Olympic champion, no world record holder ever ran so fast. The tall man moved as the wind as he literally flew up the street and snatched the small girl out of harm's way. The barest instant later the speeding SUV careened past.

Several people came out of the surrounding modest homes. One woman rushed to gather her small daughter up in her arms. With nothing but perfunctory thanks she rushed inside.

"Not much gratitude there," said Chrissie Lloyd, a neighbor from across the street. The tall man said nothing. Chrissie thought he seemed disoriented. "Why don't you come inside for a minute, have a sit down and a tea or coffee?" she asked. She wasn't in the habit of inviting strange men in, but he seemed so lost. The man seemed to incline his head and Chrissie took this as a yes.

He had still not said anything, but as Chrissie ushered him inside, something seemed to brush very lightly against her mind. She dismissed it immediately.

Sitting in the lounge room and taking the proffered cup of tea, the man finally spoke, thanking Chrissie for her kindness. His gentle voice was devoid of any accent, but it seemed the voice of an educated man.

At that moment there was a small cough from behind a door. "The little nose you can see just poking around the door is my daughter Tracey," said Chrissie.

The man motioned for Tracey to come to him. "That's unusual," said Chrissie. "She won't normally come to a stranger." Tracey, perhaps six or seven years old, would have been very pretty. If it weren't for the large ugly growth on her face and neck that is.

Chrissie seemed apologetic, tears almost coming to her eyes as her daughter stepped hesitantly toward the stranger. The man motioned again, and Tracey came right up to him. He touched her so very gently on the side of her face. Chrissie thought she saw a slight glow on his hands as he did so. The growth began to visibly recede. In perhaps a few minutes, it was completely gone. The man had performed an act that was unquestionably beyond the capabilities of the best that modern medical science could offer.

Unbelieving, Chrissie gathered little Tracey in her arms and began to cry. She carried her daughter, who seemed not yet to have realized, to the nearest mirror. When the knowledge dawned on her, the little girl let out an exclamation of sheer joy. It was a sound her mother had never expected to hear.

"Has it gone completely?" asked a trembling Chrissie. "Please don't say that it will come back."

"Completely," said the man.

"How do you know?" asked Chrissie.

"I . . . I just do," he said.

"Who are you?" asked Chrissie, her voice trembling just a little.

"I don't know," replied the man. "I seem to have lost my memory."

Whatever this man really was, wherever he was really from, he seemed content to stay with Chrissie and her beautiful little daughter for the moment. Nor did either of them wish him to leave.

"I cannot remember my name," said the man later that night, "but the name Exeter is foremost among my thoughts, perhaps you could call me that?"

The man paid his way. The next day he provided Chrissie with one of several rare gems on his person. It was worth enough to mean she and Tracey would be comfortable for life. Though Chrissie protested, Exeter dismissed her protests. He seemed to view it as a minor act on his part.

The days stretched into weeks. Exeter initially spent considerable time on the internet, reading books, and watching news and current affairs programs. Soon he seemed to tire of this, as if somehow he had learned all that he needed to know. After that he seemed content to putter around the house. He turned out to be quite handy in most departments and undertook a variety of repairs and small renovations. Chrissie's deceased husband, Tracey's father, had left a good supply of tools.

Small parts of Exeter's memory were beginning to return. At first he said nothing to Chrissie or Tracey.

However one evening after Tracey was nicely tucked up in bed he confided in Chrissie.

"I am not from your world," he said.

"I think we knew that," responded Chrissie. "Your healing of Tracey, your great speed on the day we met you, and there have been other things that perhaps you thought I did not notice."

"I cannot remember anything like all the details," said Exeter, "but I believe I am the last one of a race of beings that once spanned the stars as easily as you might walk to houses in a nearby street." Chrissie remained silent.

"I do not say this to impress you Chrissie," continued Exeter, "but only to be honest with you. Also, I want to be able to speak of my dead race, and I only have you and Tracey who I can talk to."

"We always knew you were different, that there was a greatness about you Exeter," said Chrissie trembling more than a little. "Does this mean you will be leaving us now?"

Exeter moved towards her. "Not yet Chrissie, if you will continue to have me. If it helps, perhaps you could view me as a convalescent slowly recovering from a long illness. One day when I am again what I once was, then I may have to move on." Chrissie nodded and said nothing, it was just exactly as she had seen him.

"Is Exeter your real name?" asked Chrissie.

"It was my . . . my father's name, as best it can be translated into your language," replied Exeter. "My real name does not translate so well, I am proud to continue to go by the name that you have been calling me."

Tracey was fed the truth about Exeter just a little at a time by both her mother and the man who now seemed for all intents and purposes to be her substitute father. She was totally accepting of the information and probably could have taken it in larger doses.

A period of great tranquility and happiness ensued in Chrissie's household. She was, she knew, very much in love with Exeter. However, though caring and compassionate toward both her and Tracey, he did not seem to be interested in any kind of sexual relationship with Chrissie. Although his anatomy was so similar that a comfortable accommodation would have been easily possible.

Exeter had told Chrissie one night that his people had long known of Earth. Though they had never interfered, our world had interested them. It was because physiologically humankind was closer to them than any other known race. Though the stars were well populated it turned out that bi-pedal oxygen breathing humanoid races were uncommon.

"What was the name of your race?" asked Chrissie.

"The Brell," responded Exeter, knowing that in their day they were indeed the greatest race ever to have existed among the stars.

A few weeks later Chrissie awoke to find Exeter looking very ill and very tired. She spoke of calling in a doctor, but he would not have that. There was nothing an Earth medical practitioner could do for him. Worse, a doctor might notice things that he would prefer go unnoticed. Chrissie made Exeter as comfortable as she could and sat with him as he slept most of the day.

Later in the day Exeter seemed to recover some strength before lapsing back into a sleep that took him right throughout the night. He had just started to come too mid morning when Tracey called her mum from the lounge room to come and watch the TV.

On the morning news there came the most amazing story. In the twenty-four hours since the morning before, there had been no reports of anyone dying anywhere in the world. Although it would take quite some time to confirm this, early reports were that no one had been murdered, killed accidentally, died of heart attack, cancer, or from any other cause.

Chrissie, closely followed by Tracey, moved back into Exeter's bedroom. She looked at him in a weird way that was a combination of accusation, wonder and admiration. "Was this your doing? is this the reason you are now so tired?" she asked.

"I did not mean to interfere in your world," replied Exeter. "It was a test as to the extent of my recovery, and I see that I have a long way to go." Chrissie said nothing but marveled at the being before her. If a single recovering individual of such a race could do such a thing, then they must have been all but unstoppable. Still something seemed to have stopped them. She had never asked Exeter what that was and never would. He would tell her if he wished her to know.

A month later the tragedy came unexpectedly as these things almost always do. Little Tracey was killed by a stray bullet from a shooting, a totally random event that even Exeter did not seem to foresee. Chrissic was devastated and totally inconsolable. In a totally irrational but very human way she seemed to turn against Exeter rather than to seek comfort from him. It was unstated, but she thought that with all his vast capabilities he should have been able to prevent the death.

Exeter close to full recovery made a decision. To make what he hoped was a very slight alteration in human history. If his actions could bring Tracey back into Chrissie's life, then they would be justified. Or so he reasoned.

"Tracey is dead by any human definition," said Exeter, "but the essential energy force that is her, has yet to depart her physical body." Then very quietly "If you wish it, I can prevent the departure of her life force."

"What are you saying?" asked Chrissie plaintively, "that you can bring her back from the dead?"

"She is not truly dead as the Brell would understand it." replied Exeter.

To a select few doctors and nurses Tracey's recovery from her apparent death became known as the Ward 3B miracle. As her mother had wished it, the miracle did not become public knowledge. Tracey herself was not told, at least not at that time.

Only a few days later Exeter left Chrissie and Tracey for good. One cannot perform such momentous events as staying the hand of death for an entire world, even for a day, and not expect it to go unnoticed somewhere else in the Universe. Through unearthly agencies Exeter's exploits came to the attention of the very few survivors of his once great race. They came to reclaim their own.

"I have interfered more in human history than I intended," said Exeter as he prepared to leave.

"How so?" asked a tearful Chrissie.

"In saving Tracey's life I had to give of a part of myself, a part of the Brell," replied Exeter. "Tracey will become a great leader among humankind, that part of her which is now Brell will ensure this."

As he took his leave, Exeter knew that through Tracey and her offspring an aspect of his race the mighty Brell would endure.

Life wasn't Meant to be Easy!

Greater London, A Protected Housing Estate near North Brighton, 2120 AD

"What's taking you so long," asked the youth, a sense of slavering urgency in his voice. "I want to make these toff's pay for the way they laughed at me."

"It's a type 213B residential force field," uttered his companion still wearing his semi-stealth suit. "The very latest, covering the whole block, I don't think I can crack it."

Just then a high frequency alarm went off. Enough to almost burst the ear drums of anyone under twenty. Then the sting lasers hit them both, each hit equivalent to a bad wasp sting.

"Aaghh," yelled the youth.

"Let's get the hell out of here!" yelled his companion. "We can only take a few of these."

The two boys were fast, boosted by cheap but very light and efficient exo-skeletons, they were out of the immediate area in seconds and on their high speed electromagnetic bikes. They were not quite fast enough though, as the 413E series home protection android assigned to that particular residence pursued them. With its weapon on heavy stun, it seemed to mean business.

The boys both returned fire with the cheap but effective MRF machine pistols which seemed to have been around forever. These were the twenty-second century equivalent of the once famous Kalashnikov. The droid took a few hits from them, enough to slow it a bit.

If the youths thought they were free and clear, they were mistaken. Two VHS electromagnetic bikes were following them and gaining. An unattached droid from the Housing Estate Reserve was on one bike, and the Cyborg head of Housing Estate security was on the other.

This used not to be standard practice for the protected estates. It used to be that once intruders left the Estate, it was left to the public authorized law enforcers, the PALE, to apprehend them, unless capture by the Estates' security forces was considered imminent.

For several years now though, the PALE, or the constabulary as they were still quaintly called by some, had become increasingly ineffective. Often they did not respond to anything less than murder. It had become regular practice for citizenry to lie just to get PALE attendance. Now even that didn't work. Everyone was waiting for the day when the PALE stopped attending even murders.

"We'll get them another time," yelled the youth as the pursuit continued. "Maybe outside the Estate; I want them to pay."

"Let's just worry about our own arses," said his companion as a laser shot missed his right shoulder by about two centimeters. "Anyway," continued the companion, "these folk are too well protected, with the stuff they've got, they must be in the super rich—." He didn't quite finish his sentence when two lasers now on the kill setting bore through him almost simultaneously. One through his brain the other through his lungs.

So this was the kind of world that it was. Public law enforcement was increasingly irrelevant. Large numbers of usually low-tech feral youth roamed the streets day and night in gangs looking for the slightest excuse to cause trouble. Always they had endless time on their hands and were able to call quickly on seemingly unlimited numbers of their fellow young unemployed. The rich and super rich were relatively secure in both their protected housing estates and protected large employment clusters. Many of the aged pensioners were also relatively secure in public facilities almost as well protected as the better housing estates. Many of these "greys" tended not to venture out from the aged facility. If they did, they went in numbers and with droid protection.

Anyone else though—those who could afford only minimum basic security or less—was potentially pretty vulnerable. Their only real protection was the many citizen reaction groups that now existed. One or two of them were so large, so well set up that even the larger youth gangs tended to leave them alone. As for the rest—well life wasn't meant to be easy!

If something was bad enough, such as sustained youth riots, youth gang clashes with the citizen groups, or the very occasional grey frustration riots, the military would be called in. Always they came in very hard and very heavy using far more force than was necessary. They were justifying their existence perhaps, now that there were so few international wars and only limited international terrorism.

As the youth's companion died under the laser fire, the youth called it in to the PALE then sped off again. Still pursuing him, the Cyborg left the droid to front the public authority law enforcers. The PALE attended but only just. The droid explained what the youth had been up to and that was the end of it. At least they called in the garbtruck, so that the boy's body wouldn't rot in the sun. The truck would come, at least eventually it would, depending on priorities.

The youth made a quick direct brain call to friend's ahead. A trap was set in a particularly unsavory part of the metropolis with sufficient numbers that even the Cyborg was unlikely to survive. Youth were there in numbers, and someone had a military heavy duty laser. The Cyborg veered away almost at the last moment. Had he been aware of the brain call? Or was he just being cautious?

These were both considerations, but in the end he had reached the Housing Estate time based budgetary limits for this event and had to head back to the Estate.

The Southampton Reality

"Professor Gabriella Taloni?" enquired the man as he sat on the park bench opposite the attractive redhead.

"Yes," the woman hesitated, then blurted out, "as you seem to know me, would you mind telling me just exactly where we are?"

"You are in an alternate reality," answered the capable looking man displaying a three dimensional card that identified him as Field Director Stewart Chapman ARP—Alternate Reality Police. "We have to get you out of here and back to your own reality."

"I have no argument with that," said the Professor. "I see this place bears more than a superficial similarity to Southampton, England in the late 1960s, early 1970s of my reality," she continued nervously, "but it's not Southampton is it?"

"No," responded the AR policeman. "It's not."

"When I first arrived here, I thought I had merely been displaced in time," said the Professor. "There are differences though," she continued. "Some subtle, some not, and there are some technologies in evidence here that are too advanced even for my reality." Chapman said nothing.

"There's a safe house we maintain in this reality," said the Field Director. "You'll need to stay there a couple of days until we can arrange ah . . . transportation back."

As the two walked toward the safe house, an altercation of sorts broke out on the other side of the street. Passersby became embroiled in the disagreement, some trying to calm things down, others seeming to inflame things. "Don't get involved Professor," said the field director.

"You don't have to tell me that," said Taloni as they kept on walking. Further down the street Taloni looked back. The numbers involved in the altercation were now quite large and still growing; there was no sign of police of any kind.

The "safe-house" seemed like a very ordinary residence apart from a single room, which contained equipment that was anything but ordinary.

"I advise that you just stay in the house Professor, until we can arrange your transfer," said Chapman somewhat forcefully. "The less you know about this reality and the less you interact with it the better." Taloni said nothing. It was probably exactly the wrong thing to say to someone of her inquisitive nature, though she knew it was more than just advice.

The house contained a number of time pieces; several of them referenced time in the way that she knew, and several odder looking instruments appeared to reference time as it might be measured here in this reality. As she was a Professor of mathematics, it sent her mind speculating.

"Why me?" enquired the Professor. "And don't tell me it's my good looks."

"Eh?" responded Chapman.

"Don't be coy with me, Director," said Taloni. "People get lost every day in these alternate realities, and they don't send Field Directors after all of them!"

"I'm not in a position to say," responded Chapman blandly.

He wasn't about to tell her that they were acting under an absolute priority direction from the ETP—end time police. Apparently Taloni was absessen (absolutely essential) to her own reality. It was something to do with the future development of medications that will counteract galactic viruses.

Taloni had at least been able to get an indication of when she could be transferred. Two days in her Earth's reality time frame.

The relatively few staff in the safe house were polite to her but non conversational. She was encouraged but not ordered to stay in the small room assigned to her. When she ventured out, conversation was muted, and she was not allowed in the room containing all the instrumentation. She did, however, catch a muted reference to the Southampton externality and also the Southampton paradox. Not necessarily one and the same.

This reality, which reminded Taloni so much of her home town when she was a small girl, experienced periods of dark and light, but they came more frequently than the night and day she was accustomed to. During the onset of one such dark period, she briefly went outside the building and down the street a little. Though she had effectively been ordered not to leave the safe house, no one appeared to be watching her to ensure that order was enforced.

There was not so much as a single person on the streets, and it was deathly quiet. Something about it scared her to the bone, and she headed back for the safe house briefly losing her bearings. Panic set in and was made worse by a tap on the shoulder, until she realized it was Chapman. "Something tells me you won't be venturing out again," he said, not unsympathetically.

In the room assigned to Taloni, there were no media by which she could enlighten herself of aspects of this reality. No television, radio, computer, books, other written material, or what passed for these in this reality. She was advised to go on the time reference of her own reality and that the time piece in the room was referenced to Greenwich Mean Time of her Earth. Strangely though, there was a rather large black telephone in the room. It was a design reminiscent of the 1960s in her reality. She laughed at the thought that she might receive a phone call here in this place.

Taloni came out from her room later in response to what seemed to be outside noise and increased activity within the house. Chapman was nowhere to be seen. She couldn't begin to guess what he might be up to. The outside noise increased, and she was ushered back into her room, assured there was nothing to worry about.

Then the black phone rang. She was of a mind not to answer it, but the caller persisted and no one from elsewhere in the safe house came to answer it. Nervously she picked it up to hear a shrill unintelligible sound at the other end. Her inability to understand the sound seemed to frustrate the caller whose voice became even more high pitched and eventually beyond human hearing. Now very uneasy, she put the phone down.

The noise outside had become intolerable, and the seemingly unflappable occupants of the safe house had become quite agitated. There was clearly trouble of some kind from the locals outside. Then she heard what sounded like smashing glass and gunshots. No one came to reassure her.

Taloni did not know at the time, but the existence of the safe house was known to and tolerated by the decision makers in this reality within strict parameters. However, its existence or indeed, the entire concept of an alternate reality was not known to the superstitious ordinary residents. Something had spooked the locals, and the occupants of the safe house were having trouble controlling them. A condition of its tolerated existence was that weapons were not held in the safe house. Also the safe house did not seem to have any elaborate force field protection, merely triggering systems. The advanced equipment in the special room must have had other purposes.

Taloni peeked out the door and saw the occupants of the safe house in a losing physical struggle with intruders. "Damn Chapman for not being around," she thought, "and for not briefing me on the situation here." She had the distinct impression that most of the people in the house were tech types rather than soldiers or police.

It was light outside, and summoning her courage, Taloni stepped out a side door. She had decided it was as good a time as any to form an independent assessment of this reality. By her reckoning there were three hours (of her own reality time) to the next dark time. She wandered for a while, and with clothing provided by Chapman she seemed not to attract the attention of the locals.

A part of Taloni was inclined to find somewhere to lay low and wait for Chapman and his cronies to locate her. Another part of her wanted to surreptitiously explore some parts of this reality. She opted for the latter course. Besides, recent events had caused her to lose quite a deal of confidence in the alternate reality police.

When she first arrived in this reality, Taloni had noticed how very bland the people looked. Nobody really stood out, because all of them had eminently forgettable faces. Walking around again only reinforced this impression. Though diminutive, she was a fairly striking person and was concerned she might stand out.

About fifteen minutes (her reality time) into her wandering, Taloni came across the fully automated mass transit station. She got on the northbound sleek semi-tube like conveyance. Silently, frictionless, possibly utilizing lines of magnetic force, it moved out stopping frequently at closely placed small stations. This transportation system was one example of the advanced technology that seemed a little out of place in this reality.

The short journey reminded her of the train trip from Southampton to Winchester in her reality as it would have been in 1970. The conveyance rapidly emptied with the last few remaining passengers alighting at the station stop one before the apparent end of the line. Heads turned her way in genuine surprise as these passengers realized she wasn't alighting at this point.

On arrival at "Winchester" Taloni was relieved to find that the doors of the conveyance opened automatically as they had at every other station stop. There was no one evident at the modest transit station, and as she walked towards the end of the station facilities, everything beyond a certain point seemed to completely disappear. Looking down a northbound projected path of the conveyance there was exactly nothing.

The Professor repeated the exercise on the southbound train with exactly the same unsatisfactory result.

Taloni had determined to return to "Winchester" and just walk down into the nothingness north of Winchester and see what happened. However, she could sense the onset of the next dark period. No one else was onboard the conveyance, and it came to a halt at a small station stop. The doors opened automatically and stayed open for a long time as if urging her to alight. Eventually, almost reluctantly, the conveyance doors closed. It was pretty clear that this transit system didn't operate during the dark periods.

With the next period of light Taloni returned to the place or construct or externality, which looked so remarkably like part of the ancient capital of England in her reality—Winchester. Just as before the transit station was totally empty. Whether it was courage or curiosity that drove her, she started walking into the nothingness beyond the abrupt ending of the station. She just kept on walking. Nothing happened to her. She felt no pain, no breathlessness. Her own reality watch showed no elapse of time. She half wished she had a pedometer to record any distance walked in her own reality's distance units. Although she suspected the pedometer would not register any distance.

Eventually on the other side of what she would later call a discontinuity, she saw what appeared to be the rest of the transit station and, perhaps more significantly, the rest of "Winchester." Having come this far, she decided to get on the nearby transit conveyance and see where it took her. People started to get on the conveyance, and they looked if anything even blander than on the other side of the discontinuity. The end of the line was a place that could easily have been part of Basingstoke, England in 1970. However, the whole trip, the countryside, the small towns on the way, even the people, had been decidedly less real than her trip on the other side of the discontinuity.

At "Basingstoke" the town and the transit station ended in nothing just as "Winchester" had. In other words, there was another discontinuity. Having already come so far, Taloni decided to go where she supposed no man or woman from her own reality had gone before and walked on through the discontinuity. She arrived as she more than half expected on the other side of the transit station, which happened to be on the other side of "Basingstoke." Again her watch showed no elapsed time.

There though, everything seemed decidedly less real than on the other side of the discontinuity. Almost a blur. Quite wisely Taloni decided it was time to head back.

At that moment she heard a not unfriendly voice call out, "I thought I told you to stay in the safe house." A man, though more than a little blurry, who could only be Field Director Chapman approached her wagging his finger. "Well Professor, your reality transportation window has arrived," he said. "I think we had better get you back to your own reality before you discover anything else about us!"

Back in the safe house Chapman seemed quite congenial. "We can't allow you to return to your reality knowing what you do about this one," he said quite congenially.

Gabriella looked alarmed. "You are surely not going to detain me in this . . . place?" she said almost choking.

"Of course not," responded Chapman. "We will simply erase all knowledge of this reality from your mind before we allow you to return." The field Director was almost beaming.

"Not sure I care for that," said Taloni.

"There is one advantage," said her host. "You can pretty much ask us anything about this reality, and we will be happy to tell you. After all you can't take it with you. It would be nice for that inquisitive mind of yours to know something of the truth, even if only temporarily."

As they sat on a comfortable lounge in the safe house waiting for the reality window to open, Chapman began talking even before Taloni had asked any questions. It was as if he needed to.

"We don't fully understand this phenomenon," he said. "We have used advanced technologies from other realities to send people up the tube conveyance from Southampton past the discontinuities."

"Just how far did you get?" asked Taloni with undisguised interest.

"They couldn't even reach London," replied Chapman almost dejectedly.

"If of course, there is some version of London," said Taloni almost somberly.

"Oh there is," responded Chapman. "We couldn't reach it with people, but we managed to get a dimensional camera through to the outskirts and transmit a few pictures back through camera relays."

"What did you find?" asked Taloni almost breathless with anticipation.

"You don't want to know," replied Chapman. "Even though you are about to be mind wiped of all knowledge of this reality, you still don't want to know. I will spare you that," he finished.

After quite a long pause Chapman continued, "We think this whole reality is an experiment gone seriously wrong and that those responsible never came back to correct their mistake. We are basically just keeping an eye on it and trying to make sure that it stays undiscovered."

"By eliminating anyone who inadvertently slides into this reality?" enquired Taloni, her voice scolding. Chapman was silent. "Unless of course, like me, they are too important to their own reality," concluded Taloni. Again Chapman said nothing.

Finally the reality window arrived. "Better get a move on Professor," said Chapman. "Chop chop now, you don't want to miss this."

"Just a moment," said Taloni. "What about the weird phone call I got? And the lack of activity at a night time? And the four hour light and dark? And the absence of police? And the . . . ."

Chapman seemed ready to oblige her with an answer, but she was gone before he could respond.

Professor Gabriella Taloni found herself again sitting on a park bench sharing it with a short, solidly built man of indeterminate age. She looked around and saw she was in her home town of Southampton, England. A newspaper laying on the ground indicated it was September 2008.

For just a moment she wondered what on Earth she was doing there. The short, solid man looked at her enquiringly.

She smiled at him quite expansively. "Field Director Chapman," she said. "It looks as though your mind wipe hasn't worked this time."

The Last Soldier

The huge star ships continued to gather in the remote system. Sleek, dark, and infinitely menacing they seemed, to any approaching small craft, to be of almost interminable length.

Any one of the leviathans was a world destroyer—and more. Five of them stood off Asgon the main system world. Another three stood off each of the other two inhabited planets. Four stood in reserve at the edge of the system.

It certainly seemed like overkill.

Star fighters from the defending system together with armed shuttle crafts had launched a series of attacks against the visitors. Such was the ineffectiveness of the abortive raids that they did not even evoke a response. After a number of collisions and friendly fire incidents the small crafts were withdrawn.

As yet the intruders had done nothing, apart, that is, from rendering useless almost all planetary information and communication technology systems.

From Asgon, giant, planet based, laser cannons fired off at the star ships almost continuously. Though the product of a capable technology, the unending volleys had no discernible effect on the visitors.

With impunity the aliens drew closer to each of the three populated worlds. The largest of all their vessels prepared to enter a high geosynchronous orbit above Asgon.

Though not detectable there was a sense among the planetary defenders that the great ships were readying for action.

Then with surgical precision the ship that had entered orbit destroyed with a series of energy transferences all those laser cannon that had been firing upon it. Even those located on the other side of the planet. It was an unmistakable demonstration of superior force.

Yet the leaders of this star system did not seem overly cowed. It was as if all they had done thus far was a mere going through the motions. They had to be seen to be trying to defend their world.

At that moment, this largest of all the visiting behemoths imploded. Though the entire process took no more than a single second, to observers from the planetary surface below, and just perhaps to the ships occupants, the process seemed to last an eternity.

At the same moment the other alien star ships fled the system in full teleportation mode. Though in the process two more of their number were destroyed in hyperspace in transit between jump off point and destination. It was an unmistakable demonstration of superior force every bit as convincing as that provided earlier. The only difference being that the intruders were the recipients of the demonstration.

Thousands of kilometers below a lone figure located on a small plateau towards the summit of a colossal mountain moved back inside that mountain. He/it grasped an artifact that had only one purpose. The rifle shaped weapon was not even warm, but there was no doubting, to those further inside the mountain, the part it had played in the recent destruction.

Of roughly human proportions the man, if such he was, did not seem imposing, at least not at first glance. He/it might have been a soldier from any one of a score of relatively advanced races. Though on closer inspection there was an indefinable aspect that separated him from all contemporary soldiers.

For decades, since recovering a time stasis block embedded deep within their world, the scientists of Asgon had devoted vast resources to disabling it and recovering its occupant. This ultimate soldier, last surviving member of the great race of the Brell, was the result of their labours. Or so they thought. In truth his release from the time stasis field was in response to the coming threat rather than Asgon scientific expertise.

In a time when the great contemporary civilisations were not yet aborning, lone or small groups of soldiers, such as this one, had been teleported from the Brell homeworld across the length and breadth of the cosmos. They were often times all that stood against invading star ships and even entire star fleets. For the Brell the term foot soldier held an entirely different meaning to that which is in common usc today.

At first Brell soldierly were periodically rotated back to the homeworld. Later, in their twilight, the mighty Brell sent soldiers out with time stasis blocks and a knowledge that they would not return. Some soldiers used the stasis fields and some didn't.

This particular soldier, the last one of all, was just doing what he had been trained to do, albeit it millions of years ago.

With his work done the last soldier of the Brell, no doubt to the disappointment of those he saved, re-entered the time stasis block.

At least until the next planet shattering threat arose.

The Equalizer

Detective Chris McInnes hadn't been out of her apartment in two weeks. She was under twenty-four hour protection and heavy medication since being raped by the alien shape-shifter.

Chris was probably one of the tougher cops the Big Apple had to offer, male or female. Still no one should have to experience what she did, even once, let alone twice, and she couldn't be sure that the shifter might not come back.

Chris's cell phone rang; it was her NYPD lieutenant in the sixth precinct, Verne Dumarest. "Chris?" he enquired. "There's something I think you should see; it might give you some piece of mind. We think it's your shifter," he added. "It's as dead as Julius Caesar."

Within minutes two detectives from her own precinct picked her up, and they drove out to the abandoned warehouse district.

The sight that greeted them was not a pretty one. The shifter had been badly beaten by someone who seemed to know a hell of a lot about shifter anatomy. Lieutenant Dumarest hadn't come across many shifters, but he knew that when they died, they reverted to their normal form.

"The only shifter I ever saw was the one that raped me," said Chris. "It's hard to tell with this one, because its head is so badly beaten."

"Who could have done such a thing to a shifter?" asked one of the uniform police officers.

"We are thinking another shifter," said Verne Dumarest. "Since they are usually too fast and too strong for a human."

"Unless there's a superman out there!" said the uniform, almost chuckling.

"There is one rather odd thing," said the uniform. "A man was shot dead in one of the old warehouses about a mile from here, we think a little before the shifter was killed. The dead man's been identified as a known IRA operative, sus-pected of killing British troops in one of the last acts of vio-lence in Northern Ireland," finished the uniform.

Dumarest looked directly at Chris. He could see she was warming to the situation, coming out of herself. Relief that this was probably the alien who raped her was mixed with curiosity as to who or what could have killed it.

"What do you think lieutenant?" asked Chris, "that the two events are related?"

"Uniform is just mentioning it," responded the lieuten-ant.

Just then another of the uniformed policemen brought in a scarecrow of a youth who claimed to have witnessed events.

"It looked like an accidental encounter," said the strangely erudite youth. "Both came from different directions, the shifter just as surprised as the man. It was over fairly quickly." The youth continued, "The shifter was fast, damned fast, as they all are, but the man, well . . . ." The youth hesitated for a moment, then went on nervously and less erudite. "I aint never seen anything like that before . . . . Never heard of a man beating a shifter."

Chris was thoughtful as Dumarest drove her home in his squad car. "The British might have taken out the IRA man," said Chris.

"Could be," replied Earle noncommittally.

"I heard they are still hunting the worst IRA men down," persisted Chris. "Sort of the way the Israeli's kept after the Nazis."

"I think I heard something about that," replied Verne Du-marest, sounding a bit vague.

"SAS men," said Chris still persisting. "The best of the SAS, that's who they send to hunt the worst of the IRA down."

"You don't suppose?" ventured Chris.

"Couldn't be," replied Dumarest seeing exactly where her line of thought was taking her. Somehow he didn't sound that convincing.

Chris went quiet for a while. The car was not far from her apartment now. "Do they have anyone that good?" She almost whispered, "The SAS I mean, someone good enough to take down a shifter?"

"How would I know?" said Dumarest, almost angrily, but his voice carried no conviction in it.

As Dumarest looked for a parking space near her apartment, his phone rang. He parked and motioned for Chris to stay in the car as he answered the call. It was mostly a one way conversation. The caller talking and Dumarest listening, nodding, and saying yes at the right moments.

After the call the lieutenant looked over at Chris. "No reason to carry the shifter investigation any further." He smiled. "We are not going to convict anyone for killing a shifter. I hear they are not going to look too closely at the death of the IRA man either." He added this, almost as an after thought.

Chris smiled back and went to get out of the car.

"Oh, and McInnes." Dumarest smiled again. "Your half baked ideas about some sort of SAS superman?"

"Yes?" asked Chris.

"Just keep them to yourself, won't you?"

Lightning Source UK Ltd.
Milton Keynes UK
UKOW051328061211

183293UK00002B/219/P